This book belongs to

....

Puss in Boots

make
believe
ideas

A mean old miller died one day,
and written in his will,
he gave two sons the house and horse,
while the cat was left to Bill.

Bill asked his brothers, "Can't you help?"
    (He was in a tricky spot.)
But they said, "Go! And take that cat,"
    leaving Bill with not a lot.

Bill said, "Oh, what can I do?
Perhaps I'll eat my cat!"
But the crafty cat, on hearing this,
said, "Hey! Please don't do that!"

Said Puss, "Buy me a bag and boots —
    I'll make your dreams come true.
Trust me, and I will bring you gold,
    a wife and a palace too."

Thrilled, Bill found a bag and boots.
Then Puss said, "Here's the plan:
we'll take some gifts to please the king —
and make you a wealthy man."

Puss caught a rabbit in the bag,
and then he made a stew.
"I'll take this to the king," he said,
"and say it comes from you."

Puss gave many gifts this way –
delivering them by hand.
He told the king, "They're from Lord Stone!"
(To make young Bill sound grand.)

"Now," Puss said, "trust me once more.
Go take a morning swim."
And while Bill swam, Puss stole his clothes –
which put Bill in a spin!

Just then the royal coach came past,
    so Puss said with a grin,
"Sire, Lord Stone's been robbed by thieves!"
    Said the king to Bill, "Come in!"

The princess gave Bill smart new clothes,
    and to thank her for this kindness,
Puss said, "Sire, at Lord Stone's home
    we've a feast for you and Her Highness!"

Puss had one thing left to do.

He ran ahead to find

a palace lived in by a troll –

the mean and nasty kind.

ROAR!

This troll could change into a bee,

a lion or a seal.

Puss thought, "If I can trick the troll,

his palace is mine to steal."

Said Puss, "Now, Troll, I hear it's true
you can be a lion or bee.
I picture you as a fierce beast,
but it's a MOUSE I'd like to see."

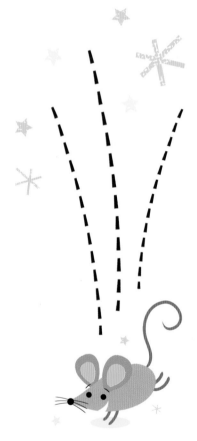

With that, the troll became a mouse —
right there on the floor!
In a flash, Puss ate him up
and wrote "Lord Stone" on the door.

Lord Stone

Lord Stone

Puss stood proudly at the door
as the royal coach arrived.
The king was amazed and said to Bill:
"Take my daughter as your bride!"

Bill had all that he could want
with a palace and his wife.
And Puss in Boots was free to live
a long and happy life!

The End